SECRET STABLE

Unique Unicorn

JOLLY
FiSH
PRESS
Mendota Heights, Minnesota

By Whitney Sanderson

Illustrated by Jomike Tejido

Unique Unicorn © 2021 by North Star Editions, Mendota Heights, MN 55120. All rights reserved. No part of this book may be used or reproduced in any manner whatsoever, including internet usage, without written permission from the copyright owner, except in the case of brief quotations embodied in critical articles and reviews.

Book design by Sarah Taplin
Illustrations by Jomike Tejido
Illustrations on pages 35, 46, 54, 63, 65, 66–67 by North Star Editions

Published in the United States by Jolly Fish Press, an imprint of North Star Editions, Inc.

First Edition
First Printing, 2020

This is a work of fiction. Names, characters, places, and incidents are either the product of the author's imagination or are used fictitiously, and any resemblance to actual persons living or dead, business establishments, events, or locales is entirely coincidental.

Library of Congress Cataloging-in-Publication Data (pending)
978-1-63163-501-4 (paperback)
978-1-63163-500-7 (hardcover)

Jolly Fish Press
North Star Editions, Inc.
2297 Waters Drive
Mendota Heights, MN 55120
www.jollyfishpress.com

Printed in the United States of America

TABLE OF CONTENTS

Welcome to Summerville
Home of Magic Moon Stable

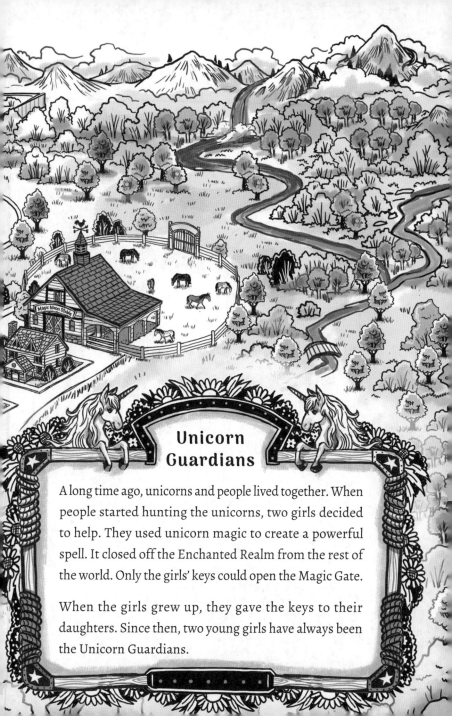

Unicorn Guardians

A long time ago, unicorns and people lived together. When people started hunting the unicorns, two girls decided to help. They used unicorn magic to create a powerful spell. It closed off the Enchanted Realm from the rest of the world. Only the girls' keys could open the Magic Gate.

When the girls grew up, they gave the keys to their daughters. Since then, two young girls have always been the Unicorn Guardians.

CHAPTER 1

Misfit

From her spot under a tree, Iris watched the unicorn stallions walk up to the stream. Both of them wanted to drink. Starfire pawed the ground. Tempest reared up on his hind legs. He was saying, "I'm bigger and fiercer than you."

Starfire took a few steps back. Tempest went up to the water. He took a long drink. When he was finished, Starfire took his turn.

A young unicorn, Galaxy, came over to drink. Starfire nipped at him as he passed.

Iris opened her notebook. *Tempest and Starfire both want to be in charge,* she wrote.

But Starfire only pretends to be fierce. He will boss around the younger unicorns, but he won't boss around Tempest. He knows that Tempest isn't afraid to fight.

"Iris, watch this!"

Iris looked up. She saw her sister, Ruby, riding on a unicorn named Moonlight Melody. They were heading toward a fallen tree. Ruby held on tightly to Moonlight Melody's mane. They cleared the tree in one swift leap.

Moonlight Melody slid to a stop in front of Iris.

"I stayed on this time," Ruby said proudly. "I'm getting better at jumping."

Iris and Ruby were both Unicorn Guardians. It was their job to look after the unicorns in the Enchanted Realm.

Ruby liked to race, explore, and have adventures. Iris was good at healing unicorns that were sick or hurt. She liked to watch the unicorns in the herd. She took notes about them. Understanding the unicorns made her feel like every unicorn was a friend.

Well, almost every unicorn . . .

Iris looked over at Lyric. As usual, the unicorn filly was by herself. She never seemed to stay with the herd. Why was she such a misfit?

Iris watched as Lyric trotted off into the Fairy Forest. Alone.

The forest was full of magic. The unicorns usually stayed out of it. Iris started to follow Lyric.

"Where are you going?" Ruby called
out. She slid down from Moonlight
Melody's back. "We have to go soon.
Aunt May is taking us to a movie tonight,
remember?"

The sun was sinking low in the sky.
Iris sighed. "Okay, I'm coming," she said,
following Ruby across the meadow. They
went through the Magic Gate together.

Iris locked it with her key. The Enchanted

Realm disappeared behind them.

Now the meadow looked like an empty pasture behind their house. The Enchanted Realm and the unicorns would stay a secret. Whatever Lyric was doing in the Fairy Forest was a secret too.

That bothered Iris. She understood most of the unicorns. But Lyric was still a mystery.

Unique Unicorn

CHAPTER 2

Dance Divas

Iris sat down at the lunchroom table. Her friends Zoey, Grace, and Kaya were already there.

"We were talking about the school talent show," Zoey said. "I think we should do a jazz routine this time."

"Our costumes should have sequins,"

Grace said. "Maybe purple sequins."

"The Dance Divas are back!" Kaya sang.

Iris took a sip of water. She didn't say anything. For the last talent show, the four of them had made a group called the Dance Divas.

Iris liked Zoey, Grace, and Kaya. But to be honest, she didn't like dancing. She felt clumsy and out of place. The other girls knew how to dance. They were good at it. Iris didn't think she was.

Iris *was* good at something else: stage magic. She had gotten a new magic set for Christmas. It would be so cool to do a magic act for the talent show.

Iris noticed someone sitting alone at the table behind them. It was the new girl, Christina. Iris had said hi to Christina earlier. But Christina hadn't looked up from her book.

Unique Unicorn

Christina reminded Iris of Lyric. She didn't seem interested in making friends. Sitting alone at lunch was Iris's worst nightmare. Iris did not want to end up like that.

But if Iris dropped out of the Dance Divas, she might end up alone at a lunch table too. Iris chewed on her sandwich, wondering what to do.

"You are quiet today, Iris," Zoey said. "Aren't you excited about the talent show?"

Iris forced herself to smile. "Totally," she said.

She tried to believe it. Maybe learning a new dance wouldn't be so bad.

"Iris, are you okay?" Kaya asked.

"I think so," Iris said. Her knee felt sore. She had been trying to do a spin that ended in a jump. Instead, it had ended in a crash.

Zoey stopped the music. Grace helped Iris to her feet.

"Should we try again?" Iris asked. She didn't want to, though.

The doorbell rang. Iris looked out the

window of Zoey's living room.

"My mom is here," Iris said.

"We can practice more tomorrow," Zoey said.

Iris was glad her mom was early. She didn't want to try the dance again. Not today, not ever. But she told her friends she would see them tomorrow.

When Iris got home, she went to her room. She took out her magic set. She made a quarter multiply until she had

two dollars. She made a birthday candle

disappear in her hand, then reappear.

She pulled her stuffed cat, Luna, out of

her magician's hat.

Iris heard clapping from the doorway. Ruby was standing there.

"You're so good!" Ruby said. "You should do your act for the talent show. There are so many people who sing or dance. Nobody else does magic."

"But I don't want to be like Lyric," Iris said.

"Huh?" Ruby asked.

"Never mind." Iris put her magic set away. She got out her homework. Her teacher had given the class five vocabulary words to learn.

"Unique," Iris read out loud. "Unlike anything else. One of a kind."

Unique seemed like a good thing. Like a magic act in the talent show.

But to Iris, it also sounded like someone who ate lunch all alone.

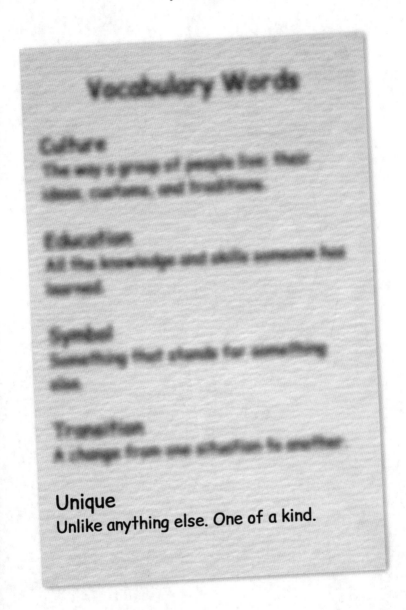

Vocabulary Words

Culture
The way a group of people live their ideas, customs, and traditions.

Education
All the knowledge and skills someone has learned.

Symbol
Something that stands for something else.

Transition
A change from one situation to another.

Unique
Unlike anything else. One of a kind.

CHAPTER 3

Lyric's Secret

The next day, Iris grabbed her notebook and a pen. She was going to solve the mystery of Lyric.

But Lyric was not easy to find. It was a hot, sunny afternoon. The other unicorns were resting in the shade. Not Lyric.

Iris searched all over. Finally, she spotted a spiral horn sticking out of the pond. Lyric was almost completely underwater. Only her head stuck out.

Lyric stayed in the cool water until close to sunset. Then she walked off toward the Fairy Forest again. This time, Iris went after her.

Lyric jumped easily over streams and fallen logs. It wasn't so easy for Iris. She was out of breath by the time she caught up. She picked a caterpillar out of her hair.

Lyric had stopped in a mossy clearing. In the center was a large tree. Its branches were bare. Iris thought it must be dead. Why had Lyric come here?

The shadows were getting longer. It would be dark soon. Iris didn't want to be in the Fairy Forest at night. She was about to turn around and go back to the meadow.

Then a yellow butterfly appeared. It fluttered across the clearing and landed on a branch of the tree. Soon, a blue butterfly joined it. Then a white one. Now the air was filled with butterflies.

It seemed like the tree was their home. The butterflies were returning for the night. They must have come from all over the Enchanted Realm.

Iris walked over to Lyric. She put a hand on the unicorn's neck. Lyric's hair was still damp from the pond.

"You knew this was here," Iris whispered. "You found it."

They watched as more butterflies appeared. The tree was not bare anymore. Its leaves were made from hundreds of living butterflies.

The light faded from the clearing. The butterflies closed up their wings for the night. Lyric knelt down on one knee so Iris could climb onto her back. They went back to the meadow together.

Later, Iris wrote in her notebook.

Lyric does not follow the same path as the other unicorns. She makes her own trail instead. At first, I didn't understand why. Then I decided to follow Lyric. She led us to a beautiful and magical place.

The next day, Iris walked up to Zoey, Grace, and Kaya after school. "I can't practice with you today," she said.

"What's wrong?" Zoey asked. "Does your knee still hurt?"

It would be easy to fib. If Iris said she was hurt, her friends couldn't be mad. But it was only fair to tell them the truth.

"I can't dance because I would rather do a magic act for the talent show," Iris said.

"You don't want to be a Dance Diva anymore?" Grace asked.

"I'm sorry," Iris said. "I like hanging out with you guys. But I don't like dancing."

"Okay," Zoey said. She looked a little hurt.

"Can I still eat lunch with you?" Iris asked.

"Of course," Kaya said. Grace nodded.

Zoey shrugged. "We like dancing, not magic," she said. "I'm not sure how much we have in common now."

Zoey's mom pulled up in her car. Zoey and the other two girls got in. The car pulled away, leaving Iris behind.

Iris felt relieved, but also sad. She hoped that being unique was worth it.

CHAPTER 4

Talent Show

Iris put on her magician's hat. "This feels too tight," she said. "I think something is in here."

She took off the hat and turned it over. A rubber mouse fell into her hand. The audience laughed.

Iris put the hat back on. "Nope, still doesn't fit." She turned over the hat a second time. A ball of yarn fell out.

"That is strange," Iris said. "I don't even knit."

She tried on the hat again. It still didn't fit right. This time, she reached inside and pulled out Luna.

"I knew it," she said. "I thought I had ordered a magician's hat. I must have ordered a magician's *cat* by mistake."

The audience clapped. Iris took a bow

and left the stage.

Her act had gone perfectly. Well, except when the playing card she had hidden up her sleeve fell out. She would have to keep working on that trick.

The Dance Divas were up next. There were still four of them: Zoey, Grace, Kaya, and Christina. Christina was a good dancer. She didn't fall when she did the spin that ended in a jump.

When the show was over, the Dance Divas came over to Iris.

"Your magic act was great," Kaya said.

"How did you pull that stuffed cat out of your hat?" Grace asked.

"If I told you, it wouldn't be magic," Iris said. She winked, and the other girls smiled.

"Christina took your place in the Dance Divas," Zoey said. Like Iris couldn't see that for herself.

"We are having a sleepover at my house tonight," Christina said.

"Oh." Iris started to turn away. Now Christina had friends, and Iris was the misfit. Suddenly her magic act didn't seem so great.

"Do you want to join us?" Christina asked. Grace and Kaya quickly nodded and begged Iris to join.

Iris whirled around. "I would love to,"

she said. "I will ask my mom."

Iris started to go over to her family. Then she turned back to Christina.

"I said hi to you at lunch last week," Iris told her. "But you kept reading your book. I thought you didn't want to be friends."

Christina blushed. "I thought you were talking to someone else," she said.

Iris had been wrong about Christina

too. She wasn't a misfit. She was just shy.

Iris's mom said she could go to the sleepover. Iris did an encore of her magic act at Christina's house. She showed the other girls how to pull Luna out of the magician's hat.

"I guess magic is pretty cool," Zoey said. She looked into the false bottom of the hat.

"Are you still mad at me for leaving the Dance Divas?" Iris asked.

"No," Zoey said. "I thought you should like dancing because we do. But we don't have to like exactly the same things to be friends."

"Maybe next year, all five of us could do a new act," Kaya said. "Dancing is fun, but so is trying other things."

"We could do a roller-skating routine," Christina suggested.

"Or I could teach everyone how to play the harmonica," Grace said.

"Whatever it is, we will be totally unique," Iris promised.

THINK ABOUT IT

 Lyric did not seem to fit in with the herd. And Christina did not seem to fit in with the other kids. At first, Iris thought they were misfits. What do you think?

 Iris was worried that her friendships would end if she did not dance for the talent show. Write about a time when your friends wanted you to do something that you did not want to do.

 Make a list of three of your unique talents.

ABOUT THE AUTHOR

Whitney Sanderson grew up riding horses as a member of a 4-H club and competing in local jumping and dressage shows. She has written several books in the Horse Diaries chapter book series. She is also the author of *Horse Rescue: Treasure,* based on her time volunteering at an equine rescue farm. She lives in Massachusetts.

ABOUT THE ILLUSTRATOR

Jomike Tejido is an author and illustrator of the picture book *There Was an Old Woman Who Lived in a Book.* He also illustrated the Pet Charms and My Magical Friends leveled reader series. He has fond memories of horseback riding as a kid and has always loved drawing magical creatures. Jomike lives in Manila with his wife, two daughters, and a chow chow named Oso.

RETURN TO MAGIC MOON STABLE

Book 1

Book 2

Book 3

Book 4

Book 5

Book 6

Book 7

Book 8

AVAILABLE NOW